Buckle My Shoe

AND OTHER COUNTING RHYMES

Illustrated by

KRISTA BRAUCKMANN-TOWNS

JANE CHAMBLESS WRIGHT

WENDY EDELSON

ANITA NELSON

LORI NELSON FIELD

DEBBIE PINKNEY

KAREN PRITCHETT

PUBLICATIONS INTERNATIONAL, LTD.

One, Two, Buckle My Shoe

One, two, buckle my shoe.

Three, four, knock at the door.

Five, six, pick up sticks.

Seven, eight, lay them straight.

Nine, ten, a good fat hen.

ONE FOR
THE MONEY

One for the money,
   And two for the show,
Three to get ready,
   And four to go.

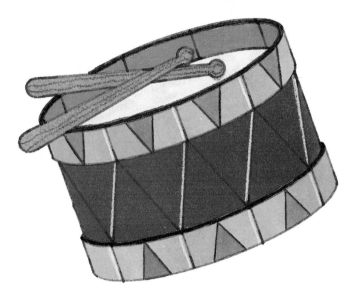

A Counting-Out Rhyme

Hickery, dickery, 6 and 7,
    Alabone, crackabone, 10 and 11,
Spin, spun, muskidun,
    Twiddle 'em, twaddle 'em, 21.

HOT CROSS BUNS

Hot cross buns! Hot cross buns!
  One a-penny, two a-penny,
Hot cross buns!

If you have no daughters,
  Give them to your sons;
One a-penny, two a-penny,
  Hot cross buns!

One to Ten

1, 2, 3, 4, 5!
   Once I caught a hare alive.
6, 7, 8, 9, 10!
   I let her go again.

THREE YOUNG RATS

Three young rats with black felt hats,
 Three young ducks with white straw flats,
Three young dogs with curling tails,
 Three young cats with demi-veils,

Went out to walk with two young pigs
    In satin vests and sorrel wigs.
But suddenly it chanced to rain,
    And so they all went home again.

One, Two, Three

One, two, three, four, five,
 Once I caught a fish alive.
Six, seven, eight, nine, ten,
 But I let it go again.
Why did you let it go?
 Because it bit my finger so.
Which finger did it bite?
 The little one upon the right.

THREE LITTLE KITTENS

Three little kittens,
    They lost their mittens.
And they began to cry,
    Oh, mother dear, we sadly fear
That we have lost our mittens.

Oh dear, don't fear,
    My little kittens.
Come in and have some pie.

THREE TIMES ROUND

Three times round goes our gallant ship,
   And three times round goes she.
Three times round goes our gallant ship,
   And sinks to the bottom of the sea.

FINGER AND TOES

Every lady in this land
    Has twenty nails, upon each hand
Five, and twenty on hands and feet:
    All this is true, without deceit.